I Don't Want to Go to Justin's House Anymore

by Heather Klassen

Illustrated by Beth Jepson

Child & Family Press · Washington, DC

If you know a child like Justin,
contact your local child abuse hotline.
In addition,
Childhelp USA maintains a national hotline: 1-800-4-A-CHILD.

CWLA Press is an imprint of the Child Welfare League of America. The Child Welfare League of America (CWLA), the nation's oldest and largest membership-based child welfare organization, is committed to engaging all Americans in promoting the well-being of children and protecting every child from harm.

CHILD WELFARE LEAGUE OF AMERICA, INC.
440 First Street, NW, Third Floor, Washington, DC 20001-2085
E-mail: books@cwla.org

CURRENT PRINTING (last digit)
10 9 8 7 6 5 4 3 2 1

Book design and production by S. Dmitri Lipczenko

Library of Congress Cataloging-in-Publication Data

Klassen, Heather.
I don't want to go to Justin's house anymore / by Heather Klassen; illustrated by Beth Jepson
    p.   cm.
Summary: Collin is reluctant to go to his friend Justin's house because Justin is being beaten by his father.
ISBN 0-87868-724-6
[1. Child Abuse—Fiction.] I. Title.
PZ7.K678144Iae 1999
[Fic]—dc21   98–47302   CIP   AC

"Mom, I don't want to go to Justin's house anymore."

But my mom just keeps on wrapping me up in layers of winter clothes, like she didn't even hear me.

"Foot," she says.

I stick one of my feet out. She slips a boot over my wool sock.

"It takes so long to get you ready to go out in the wintertime," my mom says.

"Mom, I don't want to go to Justin's house anymore," I repeat.

"Other foot," she says, but this time as she puts my boot on, she asks, "Why not? Justin is your best friend, isn't he?"

"He is my best friend, it's not that," I answer. I'm not sure how to explain it. "I want him to come play at my house. I just don't want to go there anymore."

"Hand," she says. She tugs a mitten on to one of my hands. "You know Justin's mom and I trade turns having you boys over. Other hand."

Now I'm all dressed. But I'm not ready to go.

"It's just that Justin's dad isn't very nice."

"Collin, Justin's father lost his job a little while ago. He may be in a bad mood because he's worried. Maybe you and Justin could do your best not to annoy him."

Then Mom opens the door and nudges me a little. I step out onto the porch. Mom locks the front door and then pulls on her gloves. She holds one of her hands out to me. I take it.

Justin lives down the street. Mom always walks me over. Today, I kind of shuffle. I'm in no hurry to get there. I wish my mom would understand.

"It's just that he's not very nice to Justin," I say.

"Do you mean he yells at Justin?" my mom asks.

"Well." I'm not sure how to answer that. I wish that all Justin's dad did was yell. Then maybe I'd feel better. But he does a lot worse than yell. But I'd feel like I was telling and I don't know if that's right.

"Collin, some parents yell at their kids when they get upset or they are really frustrated. That doesn't mean it's OK, but they're just not sure how to handle things better. If Justin's dad seems to yell at Justin a lot, just try to play quietly and not bother him. I'm sure he's worried about his job."

"Well," I say again. I want
to explain it to her better, but
now we're in front of
Justin's house.

I guess I'm stuck. I walk slowly up
the path to Justin's front porch. Almost
as soon as I ring the bell, Justin opens
the door.

"Hi, Collin, come see what I made for
our space station."

I turn around to look
at my mom one more time.
She waves to me.

I go into Justin's house. I sit down to pull my boots off.
"Is your dad here?" I ask.

"He's in the basement, I think," Justin answers. "Take your
stuff off fast and we can go to my room before he comes up."

I tear off my hat and coat and leave all my stuff in a pile.
Justin and I run up the stairs to his room. He closes the door.

"Look what I built."
Justin points to a tower of
wooden blocks on the floor.
"It's great," I say. I kneel
down to get a better look.

The door opens a crack. Justin and I whirl around to see who it is. Justin's mom sticks her head in.

"Hi, Collin, I'm sorry I didn't meet you at the door. I was working on my computer and didn't hear you come in. Justin, let me know if you boys need me or if you want a snack."

"OK, Mom."

Justin's mom leaves and we get back to work on the space station. We're going to make it even taller.

We work for a long time, hardly talking because we're concentrating so hard.

"I'm hot," says Justin. He stands up and pulls his sweater off over his head. That makes his T-shirt go up too. I see a big black-and-purple bruise on his back.

"How'd you get that bruise?" I ask.

Justin tugs his shirt down. "Oh, I fell. Let's get back to work."

I don't think Justin got that bruise from falling.
But I don't say anything.

We keep on building and changing things on our space station. Justin and I both want to be astronauts when we grow up.

"I wonder if our real space station will look like this," Justin says.

"Probably," I answer. I'm just about to add another block when the door opens. It's Justin's dad.

"I told you to clean up that mess in the living room," he yells at Justin.

"I'm sorry, I forgot," Justin answers.

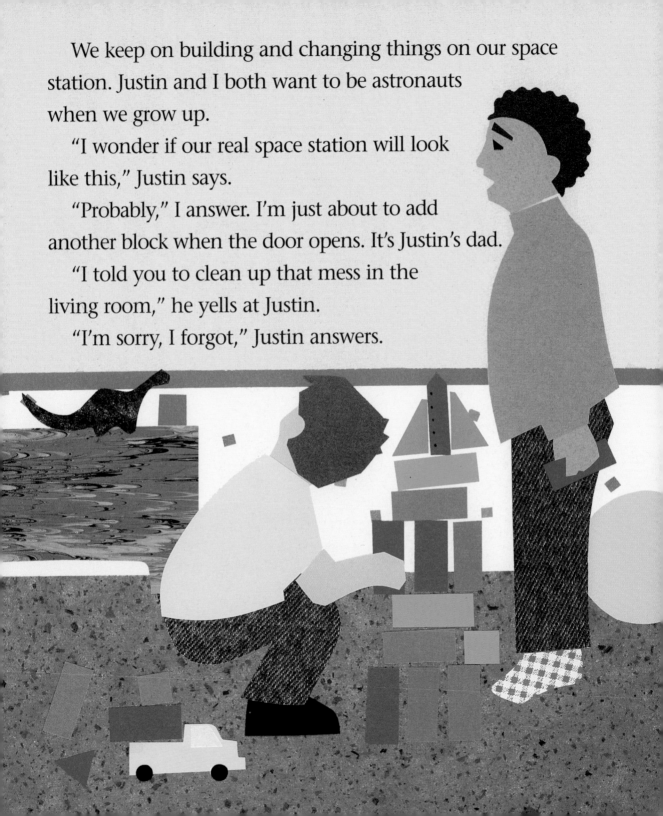

"I don't care if you forgot, you're going to clean it up right now," his father replies. He steps over to Justin and yanks him up from the floor by one arm. The blocks Justin had in his hand clatter onto the floor.

"No, Dad, don't!" Justin cries, but his dad doesn't listen. Justin's father drags him out of the room. I can hear Justin pleading with him all the way down the hall.

Now my stomach feels awful, like I'm going to throw up. I don't want to stay here. I know there will be a lot of yelling and crying and maybe even hitting sounds. After a while, Justin will come back to his room, his eyes red from crying and maybe with marks on his face. Then we'll keep on playing like nothing happened. Except that my stomach will keep feeling sick, probably until I go to bed tonight.

This time, though, I decide I'm going to leave. I creep to the door and look down the hallway. It's empty. I sneak down the hall. As I get closer to the front of the house, the yelling and crying get louder. Even Justin's mom is yelling now, but I'm not sure who she's yelling at. I know no one will notice me.

I reach the entry and see the phone on a table near the door. I pick up the receiver and press the buttons with the numbers on them. My mom answers.

"Mom, come get me," I say.

"Collin, it's only three-thirty. Is everything OK?"

"No. Please come get me," I say again.

"OK, I'll be right there," she promises.

I hang up the phone, pull on my boots, and pick up my coat, hat, and mittens. I slip out the front door. Even out here, I can hear the yelling and other sounds. I go to the bottom of the steps and wait for my mom.

She arrives right away, just like she said she would. I hurry down the path to meet her.

"Collin, what's wrong? Did something happen?"

"It was Justin's dad again."

My mom kneels down and looks right at me. "Collin, what do you mean? Was he yelling again?"

I think that now I should really tell her. I can't stop Justin's dad, but maybe if I tell my mom, she can do something. I don't know if it's right to tell, but I want Justin to be OK.

"Justin's dad hurts him."

My mom stares at me. Then she looks at Justin's house, then back at me.

"I'm sorry I didn't understand what you were trying to tell me before," my mom says.

"That's OK," I answer. "But I don't want to go to Justin's house anymore."

"You don't have to, Collin. But we need to help Justin."

"Is there something you can do, Mom?" I ask.

"Yes," she answers. "I'll make the call today to someone who can help Justin and his parents."

She stands up and takes my hand in hers. "Let's go home."

As we walk toward our house, my hand gets warmed up in my mother's glove. I decide I'm glad I told. Now maybe Justin will be OK. And we can grow up and be astronauts together.